Dear Parents:

Congratulations! Your child is taking the first steps on an exciting journey. The destination? Independent reading!

STEP INTO READING® will help your child get there. The program offers five steps to reading success. Each step includes fun stories and colorful art or photographs. In addition to original fiction and books with favorite characters, there are Step into Reading Non-Fiction Readers, Phonics Readers and Boxed Sets, Sticker Readers, and Comic Readers—a complete literacy program with something to interest every child.

Learning to Read, Step by Step!

Ready to Read   Preschool–Kindergarten
• big type and easy words • rhyme and rhythm • picture clues
For children who know the alphabet and are eager to begin reading.

Reading with Help   Preschool–Grade 1
• basic vocabulary • short sentences • simple stories
For children who recognize familiar words and sound out new words with help.

Reading on Your Own   Grades 1–3
• engaging characters • easy-to-follow plots • popular topics
For children who are ready to read on their own.

Reading Paragraphs   Grades 2–3
• challenging vocabulary • short paragraphs • exciting stories
For newly independent readers who read simple sentences with confidence.

Ready for Chapters   Grades 2–4
• chapters • longer paragraphs • full-color art
For children who want to take the plunge into chapter books but still like colorful pictures.

STEP INTO READING® is designed to give every child a successful reading experience. The grade levels are only guides; children will progress through the steps at their own speed, developing confidence in their reading.

Remember, a lifetime love of reading starts with a single step!

Step into Reading, Random House, and the Random House colophon are registered trademarks
of Penguin Random House LLC.

Visit us on the Web!
StepIntoReading.com
randomhousekids.com

Educators and librarians, for a variety of teaching tools, visit us at RHTeachersLibrarians.com

ISBN 978-0-7364-3623-6 (trade) — ISBN 978-0-7364-8230-1 (lib. bdg.) — ISBN 978-0-7364-3624-3 (ebook)

Printed in the United States of America   10 9 8 7 6 5 4 3 2 1

The Cookie Boogie

adapted by Melissa Lagonegro
based on an original story by Kathy Ellen Davis
illustrated by the Disney Storybook Art Team

Random House 🏠 New York

Pumpkin gets ready
for her big dance show.
She checks her list.
She still needs treats
for the guests.

Berry makes cookies
for Pumpkin's show.
Treasure helps.
She gets the sprinkles.

Treasure grabs
sparkly green sprinkles
from the cupboard.

Berry shakes sprinkles

on the cookies.

The sprinkles sparkle

and swirl!

They are magical.

The cookies come to life!

The cookies march
out the door!
Berry and Treasure
are shocked!

Ms. Featherbon says
the sprinkles are
her lost magical
glitterbits.

Berry and Treasure
hear a noise.
Pumpkin needs help!

The cookies are
out of control.
They might ruin
her dance show!

Berry and Treasure
chase the cookies.
Berry tries
to catch one.

The cookie gets away.

Berry gets messy.

Treasure follows
a cookie up a tree.
She jumps
toward the cookie.

The cookie jumps
to another branch.
It gets away!

Pumpkin practices
her dance moves.
The cookies watch her.
They dance, too!

The cookies
follow Pumpkin.
They dance
into Berry's basket.

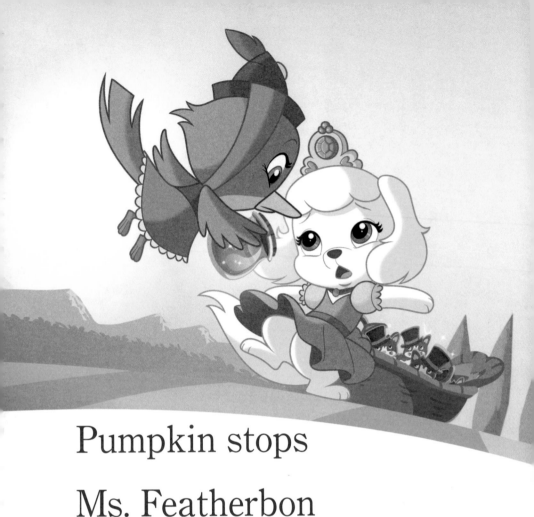

Pumpkin stops
Ms. Featherbon
from changing
the cookies back.
She wants them
to dance in her show!

It is showtime.

Everyone is seated.

Pumpkin starts
to dance.
The cookies dance
with her.
The show is a big hit!

The pets and the cookies
make a great team.
What a fun
cookie boogie!